Three Weeks
in Utica

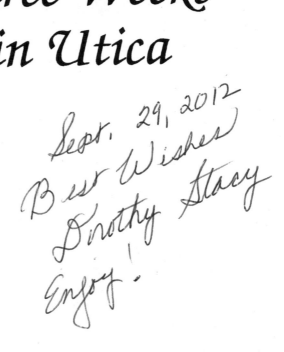

Sept. 29, 2012
Best Wishes
Dorothy Stacy

Enjoy!

Three Weeks
in Utica

by
Dorothy Stacy

August 1840						
Sun	Mon	Tue	Wed	Thu	Fri	Sat
						1
2	3	4	5	6	7	8
9	10	11	12	13	14	15
16	17	18	19	20	21	22
23	24	25	26	27	28	29
30	31					

Blackberry Hill Press
Sauquoit, New York

Library of Congress Control Number: 2008903690

ISBN: 978-0-9792947-1-6

Illustrations by the author
Cover image: William H. Bartlett's
Sketch of Genesee and Washington Streets in 1838
Source of the original image
Oneida County Historical Society
Utica, NY

Published by
Blackberry Hill Press
2860 Mohawk Street
Sauquoit, New York
Email: dhstacy@gmail.com
Website: dorothystacy.com

Printed in the U.S.A. by
Morris Publishing
3212 East Highway 30
Kearney, NE 68847
1-800-650-7888

"...No country like America,
No state like New York,
No county like Oneida,
No city like Utica."
--Roscoe Conkling

Also by Dorothy Stacy:

Erie Canal Cousins--- April 2007

This book is dedicated to....
My grandchildren,
Kyle, Katelyn, Kathryn, Kurt, Julia, Olivia,
Jack, Tanner, Mason, Hunter, Haley, Andrew,
Michael, Austin, James,
and my uncle, Walter Lewandowski

Special thanks to...

My husband, Jack, who listened to me read and talk about the manuscript and is my strongest supporter. I love you.

Janet Davis, my good friend, for taking the time to read my manuscript, comment on it, and do some editing of it. Thanks a bunch!

My Uncle Walt for teaching me all I know about working with pictures on the computer. I never could have done it without you!

Nancy Rand, my neighbor, and Karen Tucker, my daughter, for graciously volunteering to edit the manuscript for me.

My daughter, Kathy Alsante, for reading and commenting on the manuscript.

All of the schools, historical societies, libraries, and clubs for inviting me to present my first book to them.

The children and people that have read my book, loved it, and urged me to write the sequel to it. As a result, Erie Canal Cousins is now a series.

The great staff at Morris Publishing for being helpful and supportive every time I called. You are the best!

Brian Howard, Executive Director of the Oneida County Historical Society, for all the help given in providing a print for the cover of the book and carrying my book in the bookstore.

Thank You, Everyone!

Author's Note

There are many books written about the history of Utica for adults, but I have never seen one for children. Because of that, I decided to write this book to help youngsters become aware of the fascinating history of this area in another historical fiction novel.

Three Weeks in Utica is the continuing story of Rose Stewart from my first book, **Erie Canal Cousins.** In this new book, you will meet Rose's other cousins the Millers, a new friend Maggie, and Maggie's brothers, Seth and Samuel. You will discover many interesting stories and surprises about early Utica history throughout the book.

Many children and people have asked me what happens to Rose next and encouraged me to write a sequel to my first book. After much thought, I decided not only would I write the sequel, but would expand **Erie Canal Cousins** into a series.

Three Weeks in Utica is fiction; however, the happenings are typical of events of that period. The characters are fictitious, but I did use some of my grandchildren as models for the illustrations. Utica is a real city, where I have lived half of my life, and the facts about it are true to the best of my knowledge. After two months of research for this book, I have become so addicted to Utica history; I can't stop reading about it. I♥Utica!

Tip—If you read through the **1840's Sayings (in the back of the book on page 93) first, when you come to one of these words or phrases in the story, you'll know what they mean.

Contents

Rose Stewart

Chapter 1
Utica Cousins

Tuesday, August 11, 1840
Utica, New York

I awoke with a start this morning at the shrill sound of a rooster crowing. For a moment, I could not remember where I was. I was not at home in my bed in Albany. Nor was I still in the cabin of Uncle Dermot's boat on the Erie Canal. The smell of freshly cut hay drifted through the open window, and cool air had replaced the stifling heat of the night before. As I glanced around the room, I finally remembered that I, Rose Stewart, was now in Utica on my Aunt Jenny and Uncle Andrew's farm. I will be here for three weeks to help Aunt Jenny with the boys and the new baby.

I am writing about my adventures on this trip in the journal my mother gave me for my thirteenth birthday, a few months ago. It was late when Uncle Andrew brought me here from the boat last night. Still, I was able to meet the boys and have a glimpse of the baby. They were in their nightclothes, but Aunt Jenny allowed them to stay up until I arrived.

Jared, the oldest boy, is six. He is tall and thin and seemed to be quite timid as he stayed close to his mother's skirt. Benjamin, the four-year-old, is friendly and giggled a lot. The two-year-old, George, named after George Washington, is as cute as a button and raised his chubby arms to have me pick him up as soon as he saw me. After they met me, Uncle Andrew whisked them off to bed.

It was then that I met sweet Willie, the baby. His real name is William but Aunt Jenny said everyone calls him Willie. He is three weeks old and so very tiny. With that lively group, I can see why Aunt Jenny needs the help. Soon after that, we all retired for the night.

My trip here on the Erie Canal was very exciting, although it did not start out that way. I was supposed to go with Mama, but my little brother broke his leg the night before, and I ended up going without her. I am timid and not very outgoing, so I was frightened and did not want to set out alone, but Papa convinced me that I would enjoy the Grand Canal and Utica. He and Mama told me...

"Wa-a-a-a-a-a." The sound came from down the hall. Rose put aside the journal she was writing in and tiptoed in the direction of the sound.

"Wa-a-a-a-a." There it was again. It seemed to be coming from the large room at the end of the hall. When

2

she peeked in, Rose saw Willie, stirring in the cradle at the foot of the bed. He was so little and so beautiful. She cautiously wandered in and lifted him up. That seemed to make him cry louder, and he rooted around looking for his breakfast.

"Shhhh," Rose panicked and tried to quiet him, but his cry soon woke Aunt Jenny.

"Oh, Rose. You startled me," she said rubbing her eyes.

"I'm sorry. I didn't mean to wake you." Rose was still in awe of how much Aunt Jenny looked like her mother. They were sisters but *not* twins. However, the resemblance was incredible. They were both tiny, had red hair, green eyes, and very similar mannerisms.

Rose herself looked more like her father. Her hair was coal black, long, and as straight as string. Her blue eyes were the color of the sea, and she was tall and big boned. She always seemed to be taller than many women and most girls her age.

Until Rose met her aunt, she had been dreading this new situation as much as she had dreaded the trip alone on the Erie Canal. It was this look-alike discovery about her aunt that finally enabled Rose to relax and believe that her stay in Utica would turn out fine. What's more, she had her Cousin Bridget's advice she was now going to try to live by. *Do the thing you're scared of, and the more you do it the less scared you'll be*. It did seem to help when she became frightened on the boat.

"Rose, can you bring the baby here, so I can feed him?" Aunt Jenny's words interrupted her thoughts. Her voice was just a bit louder than a whisper, and she looked very tired as she pulled herself up to a sitting position in the bed.

"Yes," Rose answered as she handed Willie over to his mother. "What can I do to help?"

"You can get the boys up and get them dressed. Uncle Andrew is already out in the field cutting the hay."

"Where are the boys?" Rose asked.

Just as Aunt Jenny was about to answer, Benjamin and George came running into the bedroom, nearly knocking Rose off her feet.

"Hello Rose!" They took turns shouting the greeting while hopping up and down.

"Boys, boys! Be quiet. Your Mama is trying to feed the baby. Come with me and I'll help you get dressed." She took one in each hand and led them down the hall. "Show me where your room is," she added.

"Here!" Little George pointed.

Jared was still in his bed, but by the time Rose had dressed the other two, he was up looking for his things.

"Would you like me to help you, Jared?" Rose asked.

"No, I can find my own things," he grumbled, turned his back on her, and started to get dressed. He didn't want to have anything to do with her.

His rude behavior puzzled Rose. She suddenly felt out of place. Children usually liked her. However, Jared had seemed shy to her. Maybe he was acting like that because he didn't know her very well. She could relate to that, being timid herself.

4

When the boys were all ready, Rose took them downstairs into the kitchen. Already there, Aunt Jenny was rocking Willie in the big rocking chair.

"Rose, it's so nice to have you here. I've been so tired since the baby came, and now I can rest knowing there's someone here to help."

"Oh, Aunt Jenny, you can count on me. I can cook quite well, and I'm very good at cleaning... and washing... and taking care of children," Rose blurted out all in one breath.

"Bless you, Rose," Aunt Jenny said. "You're just what I need. I'm going back upstairs to nap with Willie."

Rose gave the boys their breakfast, and then decided to clean the dishes and straighten up the kitchen. She felt good, knowing her aunt appreciated her help.

"Can we go outside?" Benjamin tugged at her dress.

"Outtide," echoed George.

Jared continued to keep his distance.

"Sure," said Rose. "Let's go."

She picked George up and took Benjamin by the hand as Jared lagged behind.

Outside the sky was as blue as a robin's egg without a cloud to be seen anywhere. The sun felt very warm. Beetles loudly signaled it was going to be another hot August day. It was good to be on solid ground again after four days on the boat.

George and Benjamin immediately ran to a dirt pile and began to dig and build with sticks and rocks.

5

"Jared," Rose called. "Don't you want to join the boys?"

"No!" He asserted as he stood by the door with his hands on his hips.

"What would you like to do?"

"Nothing," he said firmly, not moving an inch.

"Would you like me to tell you a story?" Rose tried to approach him.

"No, leave me alone!" He turned his back to her.

Rose was at a loss as to what to do. He was going to be a challenge.

Soon Aunt Jenny was calling her in to help make lunch. The boys stayed outside, while Rose and Aunt Jenny prepared the noonday meal.

Shortly Uncle Andrew, Joe, the hired hand, and the boys were sitting down to some ham, corn, biscuits, and loads of sweet, juicy blackberries from the farm. They had plenty of fresh milk, straight from the cows, to drink.

Rose served the family as Aunt Jenny sat in the rocker and watched. She still felt exhausted. It was so good to have some help

After lunch, George and Benjamin went up for a nap followed by Aunt Jenny and Willie. Uncle Andrew and Joe went back into the fields to work. Rose quickly ate her own lunch, and again cleaned up the dishes and straightened up the kitchen. Jared wandered outside with a warning from Rose to stay nearby. After all, she was responsible for him now that Aunt Jenny was napping.

Rose was beginning to wonder if all of her days in Utica would be like this. She was beginning to feel homesick and lonely. The heat made her sleepy and the work made her tired. Aunt Jenny might *look* like her mother, but her mother did not sleep all day, and she was fun to talk to and be around.

She glanced out the window to see if Jared was there, but could not see him. She went outside, walked to the front of the house and then to the back. Where was that child? Rose called his name several times. Her heart raced as she ran up into the field. He wasn't there either. Where could he be? She looked behind all the trees, in the shed, and in the barn. Jared was nowhere to be seen.

She would have to tell Aunt Jenny. She felt like such a failure. She couldn't even watch one little boy. Perhaps he was hiding indoors.

With a heavy heart, she started back to the house, all the while calling Jared's name. She went inside and searched the kitchen, the dining room, and the parlor. By now, her stomach was starting to tighten, and her head began to ache. Where in the world could he be?

Rose wearily climbed the stairs. She would have to tell Aunt Jenny. Wait, maybe he was in the boys' room. She crossed her fingers and peered inside. She looked under the beds and even in the toy box. No Jared. Her heart pounded faster and faster. Now she had to tell Aunt Jenny; there was no other place for her to look. Aunt Jenny wouldn't be so grateful for her being there, when she learned that Jared was lost.

Rose tiptoed into the master bedroom and was just about to call Aunt Jenny's name when she saw a surprising sight. Curled up on the bed next to Aunt Jenny and Willie, lay Jared... fast asleep. Relief flooded her body. He must have snuck upstairs when she wasn't looking. She wanted to take hold of him and shake him for scaring her so, but she was so happy to find him, she just walked out of the room. She went downstairs and remembered that it was time to start supper.

Soon everyone awoke, and the commotion started again. Rose cooked supper and everyone came in and ate. Aunt Jenny fed the baby and went back upstairs for the night. Rose put the boys to bed, straightened up the house, lit a candle, and sat down to have a nice cold mug of cider. She put her feet up on the chair next to her. Her body just ached from head to toe. She wiped the beads of perspiration off her forehead with her apron. It was still hot even though the sun had gone down. It felt so good not to have anything more to do.

She jumped when she saw something move out of the corner of her eye. It looked too big to be a mouse. Rose turned her head quickly in that direction.

"Jared! What are you doing down here?" She was surprised to see him standing there.

"I'm not tired," he stated.

"Would you like me to get you something to eat?" She remembered that he had not eaten very much for supper that night.

8

"No," he shrieked. "Why are you here?" he continued. "Are you here to take my Mama's place? I don't want you here!" He looked like he was about to cry.

"No, Jared." Rose couldn't believe what she was hearing. "I would never try to do that."

"Then why don't you go home? I can help my Mama. I'm a big boy!"

"I'm just here…"

"I hate you," Jared interjected as he ran from the room and back upstairs.

That was the last straw. Rose had never come across a child as ornery as Jared was. He reminded her of Bridget, her boat cousin. Rose felt her eyes fill with tears. She was only trying to help and this was what happened. She felt crushed inside and was soon weeping. It was not supposed to be like this. Mama said Utica would be fun. She was supposed to enjoy the children and her aunt's company. Instead, she was exhausted, Jared was impossible, and her aunt slept all the time.

The Miller Family

Uncle
Andrew

Aunt
Jenny

Jared

Benjamin

George

And the new addition....

11

Baby Willie

Chapter 2
Meeting Maggie

Wednesday, August 12, 1840

My first day in Utica did not turn out so good. The incident with Jared last night left me distressed. Aunt Jenny found me weeping at the table after he went back to bed. She came down for some water. I quickly tried to dry my tears and look composed, but she sensed my turmoil right away.

When she asked me what was wrong, all of my feelings about the day came rushing out like an erupting volcano. Through sobs, I told her everything. It felt good to get it out.

Aunt Jenny put her arms around me and let me cry on her shoulder. She then cautioned me about trying to do everything all the time and said I was allowed to rest and have some fun, too. What a relief that was. She also said that Jared was high strung and did not take easily to strangers, but would probably perk up when he got to

13

know me better. She was sorry he treated me that way and would have a talk with him about it in the morning.

I finally stopped crying and was able to retire in a much better frame of mind.

Rose

Rose put her journal away and went downstairs to begin the new day. She was determined not to get overwhelmed by things no matter what happened.

Aunt Jenny was already in the kitchen starting breakfast.

"I can do that," Rose stated, feeling guilty. "You go rest."

"Oh, no. I feel much better with all that rest I got yesterday. Thank you for taking care of things."

"All right. Then what would you like me to do?" Rose asked.

"You can set the table, and then get the boys dressed and bring them down."

"Very well. I'll be right back." Rose did what Aunt Jenny asked and soon was back with the boys. George and Benjamin squabbled about who would sit by her at the table while Jared hung back until he saw his mother. Then he rushed over to her immediately and hugged her skirt, not wanting to let her go.

After breakfast, Rose helped Aunt Jenny pick up the kitchen and then took the boys out back to play. Rose sat

14

down on the porch where she could watch them and began to write a letter to her family in Albany.

No sooner had she begun, than she saw someone coming down the road in front of the farm. As the person turned up the path and came closer, Rose saw it was a girl…a girl that looked about her age. She was tall like Rose was, had something in one hand, and was waving with the other.

"Hello there," she shouted as she left the path and walked over to the porch where Rose was sitting.

"Hello," said Rose. "Where did you come from?"

"I live on the next farm. My Mama sent me over with some molasses cookies to welcome you. We heard you were going to be here for awhile, and I reckoned you might like a friend nearby."

"Yes, yes. I certainly would." Rose could not believe her ears. That was just what she needed.

"By the way, my name is Margaret Evans, but everyone calls me Maggie." Maggie's dark brown hair was parted in the middle and neatly braided into one long pigtail that hung down her back nearly to her waist. Her eyes matched the color of her hair and danced when she spoke.

"Nice to meet you. I'm Rose…Rose Stewart."

"We heard you came here all the way from Albany."

"That's true. I came down the Erie Canal on my uncle's boat, the *Flying Eagle*."

"The Grand Canal! That must have been exciting!" said Maggie, wishing she could do that.

"Oh, that it was." Rose smiled, recalling the ups and downs of it all. "Do you have any brothers or sisters, Maggie?" she asked.

"Only two older brothers. Samuel is fifteen, and Seth is fourteen. Mama had two more boys after me. One passed away in childbirth and the other only lived for six months. She is going to have another baby this winter, and I hope this time it's a girl. The boys are always trying to protect me...too much sometimes, so I try to escape from them as much as I can. What about you?"

Rose laughed. "I have a younger sister, Cassie, who is eleven and two younger brothers, Robert nine and Caleb four."

"I wish I had a sister," Maggie said longingly.

"Sisters are good enough most times, but sometimes we fight," Rose admitted.

"If I had a sister, I would *never* fight with her," Maggie said.

Rose did not say a word, but knew from experience that would not be so.

"After I drop the cookies off, I have to go into the city for Mama to get her some salt for pickling from the Old Clinton Market. Would you like to come? We can talk on the way."

"I'll have to ask Aunt Jenny. I'll be right back."

Rose turned and ran into the house. Aunt Jenny told her she could go, but to bring the boys in before she left, and might she pick up some salt at the market for her, too. She needed to make some dill pickles.

16

Soon the two girls were walking down the dirt road towards Bleecker Street.

"What do you like to do?" Maggie asked.

"The thing I like to do best of all," said Rose, "is writing. I hope to be a writer like my Papa. He writes for the newspaper in Albany."

"Do tell. How exciting!" said Maggie.

"I also like to read and cook," said Rose.

"So do I," said Maggie. "I love to read."

"I love school and learning, especially history," said Rose excitedly, hoping she did not sound too serious.

"That's incredible. Those are exactly the things I like, too. What's more I like to grow flowers, and I *love* to swim." Maggie was thrilled that they had so much in common.

"Swimming? That's one thing I never learned to do," said Rose.

"Swimming is easy. I can show you how, some day, but not in the canal. You get fined two dollars if they catch you in there during the day."

"Uh…All right," Rose said hesitantly while her insides went weak at the thought of trying to swim.

They continued to chat as they went down Bleecker Street past Chancellor Square and there, facing Market Street, was the Old Clinton Market. It was a large two-story building where farmers sold or traded fresh meat, fruits, vegetables, hay, and firewood for groceries, salt, gunpowder or dress materials. Each butcher had a stall where his meat, poultry, or game hung on racks. Against the sides of the building, sheds housed the finest, freshest produce in the area. City homemakers and their daughters were there, picking out supplies and catching up on the gossip of the day. It was a busy, interesting place to be.

Many of the people knew Maggie and greeted her. She, in turn, introduced Rose. The girls purchased their salt, and after looking around at the many offerings, set forth for home. The day was getting hotter by the minute, but with a friend to talk to, the trip back home seemed short.

Maggie said goodbye with a promise that she would be over the next day and left Rose at the entrance to the farm. Rose was back just in time to help Aunt Jenny serve lunch. A smile kept lifting the corners of her mouth as she went about her work.

"I reckon you and Maggie took to each other," said Aunt Jenny.

"Oh, yes. Maggie is so much like me. We both like the same things, and she is going to come over tomorrow, and she wants to be friends." The words came rushing out nonstop.

"I don't reckon I've seen you so excited yet."

"It's going to be fun having a friend like Maggie." Rose was quiet through lunch, but her mind was spinning, thinking of all the great things she and Maggie would do together.

Later that evening when the boys were in bed, Uncle Andrew came in and said he had a surprise for them.

"On my way back from the city, I ran into my second cousin, Philip, and he invited us all to a social gathering on Saturday at his grandmother's mansion on Chancellor Square."

"Oh, how splendid!" gasped Aunt Jenny.

"He said the family hadn't seen us in a long time…in too long a time, in fact. So we'd better come."

"Yes, we'll go. Rose, you can come, too. I bet Maggie can watch the boys." Aunt Jenny's voice quivered with excitement. "Wait till you see the house. It is magnificent," she continued. "We'll have to get out our Sunday best and fix our hair…" Aunt Jenny sounded like a schoolgirl looking forward to her first date.

"I can't wait," said Rose. The excitement was contagious, but she felt a little queasy about meeting all of those new people. Then she remembered what her Cousin Bridget had said, *Do the thing you're scared of, and the more you do it the less scared you'll be.* Moreover, Rose intended to do so.

Maggie Evans

Chapter 3
Frolic at the Mansion

Saturday, August 15, 1840

I can't believe I have not written in this journal for two whole days. I met a new friend. She lives on the next farm and her name is Maggie. She is my age and likes the same things that I do, but she is not timid like I am. In fact, she is a little bold. She would have to be, with two older brothers telling her what to do all the time.

Maggie came over a few times after she finished her own work. She even helps me with my work when she is around. She is so easy to talk to and fun to do things with. Between that and the work around here, I just did not have the time to write. So today, I am making the time.

On the way home from the Clinton Market, I asked Maggie why Utica had such an unusual name. She said her Papa told her that Utica was first called Old Fort Schuyler. When it became a village, people decided that it should be called something else. So thirteen men met in

21

Bagg's Hotel to come up with a new name for it. They had many ideas but could not see eye to eye on one. Therefore, they decided that each person would write his choice on a slip of paper and place it into a hat. The first name drawn would be the new name of the village. It turned out to be Utica, the choice of Erastus Clark in honor of an old city in North Africa.

I reckon I like some of the other names suggested better such as Washington, Kent, or even Sconandoa. Nevertheless, Utica was the name they picked, so that is what it is.

Tonight is the frolic at the mansion in Utica, and I wish to record it all here. Uncle Andrew told me that we could ride by some of the other beautiful mansions in the city on the way to the frolic. He said Main, Broad, and Whitesboro Streets have some of the finest homes in Utica on them. Most of the well-to-do people live on Broad Street.

Benjamin and George now run up to me as soon as they see me and want me to tell them a story. Jared has calmed down some and has not had any more outbursts since his mother talked to him. I hope he finally understands that I am not trying to take his mother's place. Now he usually just ignores me. On the other hand, I did see him inching over closer when I was telling the boys a story the other day. I will keep working on it and hopefully, he will come around.

Rose

Rose put her journal away and took her dress for the frolic out of the closet. It was her one good dress. It was not the best, but it would have to do. She couldn't bring too many things with her on the boat. Aunt Jenny offered to loan her one of her dresses, but she was six inches taller than her aunt was, and it wouldn't fit.

Just then, she heard someone running up the stairs.

"Rose, I have a surprise for you." Maggie burst into the room. She was already there to watch the boys, and she was holding something in her hand.

"What is that?" asked Rose.

"It's a dress, my dress, and I want you to wear it to the frolic."

"Oh, Maggie, it's beautiful!" gasped Rose as she fingered the pale green fabric and ecru lace trim. "Will it be all right with your Mama if I wear it?"

"Yes, she said you could. She made it for my cousin's wedding, and I won't have reason to wear it much again," said Maggie.

"Oh, Maggie thank you, thank you," Rose shouted and hugged her new friend so tight they almost fell over. "I wish you could go with us."

"Me, too," said Maggie longingly.

"I'll remember everything that happens, and I'll tell you all about it tomorrow," said Rose.

"You promise? Now, put the dress on. I want to see how it looks on you." Maggie held the dress out to her.

"Sure," said Rose slipping off her own dress and putting on Maggie's. The dress fit like it was made for her. She and Maggie were about the same size.

"Let me fix your hair, too," said Maggie. She combed it back and twisted it into knot at the top of Rose's head. Then she pulled a few pieces out at the sides. "There," she said, "now you look fashionable."

Rose looked at herself in the mirror. She looked magnificent in the dress, and her hair looked like it was right out of Godey's Lady's Book. "Thank you, Maggie," she burst out and hugged her again.

"Are you ready, Rose?" Aunt Jenny's voice came from the hallway.

"Yes, Aunt Jenny. Maggie let me wear her dress, and it is just spectacular, and she did my hair, too. Come in and see."

"Why, Rose, you look dashing!" Aunt Jenny remarked when she entered the room. She turned her niece around to get a better look.

"Aunt Jenny, you look dashing, too," said Rose.

Aunt Jenny was wearing a turquoise print dress with a matching fringed shawl. Her red hair was parted in the middle and done in sausage curls that started above her ears and ended at her shoulders. It was quite a change from the nightdress or working clothes Rose usually saw her in.

"It's time to go now. Uncle Andrew has the horse and wagon ready outside," Aunt Jenny announced. After giving Maggie instructions as to what to do with the boys and the baby, Aunt Jenny and Rose left.

Uncle Andrew took them on a tour of Utica first, pointing out some of the elegant homes to Rose. "We're on Broad Street now and to the right you will see the home of Moses Bagg, and down the street a ways is the home of Samuel Stocking. The Stocking Home is one of the best designed houses in this part of the state."

"Man alive! I've never seen such beautiful houses," Rose uttered as she stared at the breathtaking sights.

Uncle Andrew turned down First Street and went over Main Street. "There on the right is the famous Bagg's Hotel that we're always talking about." He felt proud of the city he lived in and wanted to show it off.

"Maggie told me that's where they picked the name for Utica," Rose stated.

"That's true," he said. "When we cross over John and Genesee Streets, we will be on Whitesboro Street where more beautiful homes are to be found. The Horatio Seymour House and the Watson Williams House are located next door to each other, there on your right," Uncle Andrew continued as he slowed the wagon so Rose could get a better look.

"They share flower gardens in their back yards. Mrs. Seymour hands out clippings of her lovely flowers to most of the people in the area," Aunt Jenny commented.

"I reckon Mama was right when she told me Utica was a beautiful city," Rose remarked.

Uncle Andrew turned the wagon around and went back over Main Street, up First Street, and around Chancellor Square. Soon they were in front of the residence where the frolic was being held.

"Well, this is it," said Uncle Andrew. "We are here. This is the Devereux Mansion." He helped Rose and Aunt Jenny out of the wagon and tied the horse up to the post.

Rose's eyes widened at the sight of the mansion. It was an enormous two story, red brick structure near the road with a beautiful flower garden to the right of it. Aside of the garden was a high brick wall for privacy. Every room in the house was alight with candle glow, and they could see people chatting indoors and out in the garden.

Uncle Andrew lifted the big brass knocker and thumped on the front door. Soon a girl a little older than Rose opened it and welcomed them in.

"Good evening, Sir, Madam, Miss," she said as she curtseyed. "Come in and join the party. There are hors d 'oeuvres in the parlor and some out in the garden."

"Good evening," said the three guests.

The magnificence of the room fascinated Rose. Elaborate white moldings crowned the tall ceilings; candle-lit crystal chandeliers adorned each room; gold flocked wallpaper from France and brocade drapes added to the splendor of the residence.

"Isn't it lovely?" Aunt Jenny sighed.

"I've never seen such a beautiful house," said Rose. "Who was that girl at the door?" she added.

"That was one of the servants," said Uncle Andrew. "It takes a lot of help to keep up a house and grounds like this. They actually have five servants who take care of the gardening, cleaning, cooking, and help with the children."

Another young girl entered the room and announced, "Dinner will be served in half an hour."

Uncle Andrew went to look for his cousin Philip, and the ladies tasted some of the delicious treats laid out on the lace-covered tables. Aunt Jenny introduced Rose to the women that were there, and then took her out to the garden where she met more of Uncle Andrew's relatives and friends. Everyone was happy to meet her. Rose began to relax, with Aunt Jenny at her side and the soothing quality of the garden.

"The flowers are so lovely. They look like bouquets from heaven." Rose could not take her eyes off the huge variety of blossoms and their vivid colors. Pink, white, and red hollyhocks together with white snowballs grew near the wall. Several types of roses, lemon lilies, and four-o'clocks were in the middle. Violets, myrtle, and alyssum filled in the front, while cascades of spirea beautified the edges. Rose was amazed to see so many flowers, all in one place. There was also an herb garden and another garden full of vegetables and fruits.

"These gardens are some of the best in Utica," Aunt Jenny remarked.

"I can see why," said Rose. "They truly are outstanding."

Walks, edged by purple and white fraxinellas, led through the many different parts of the grounds. Lilac bushes, some pine trees, and many elegant elms beautified the back of the estate.

The girl who answered the door now rang a little bell and said, "Dinner is served."

Everyone started toward the house and headed in the direction of the dining room. Aunt Jenny and Rose looked for their name cards on the table.

"Over here," Uncle Andrew said as he motioned from the other end when he saw them. "We're all together down here." The ladies took their seats next to him.

"Did you have a nice chat with your Cousin Philip?" Aunt Jenny asked.

"Oh, yes. We caught up on all of the family news. I'll bring you up to date when we get home."

The dining room table was covered with the finest damask tablecloth. Matching damask napkins, English bone china, sterling silverware and candelabras, as well, added to the graciousness of the look. In the center was a huge bowl of fresh cut flowers from the gardens.

If this is what the table looks like, I wonder what the dinner will be like, Rose thought.

As if reading her mind, Uncle Andrew said, "This will probably be a seven course dinner, so don't eat too much of any one thing."

"Seven courses?" gulped Rose. "I hope I can eat all of that food."

"Eat slowly and just a little of each thing. If I can do it, you can too," coaxed Aunt Jenny. "The food will be delicious."

The first servant girl brought out corn chowder, after which a delicious, roast wild turkey delighted their taste buds. Next, there were boiled onions, buttered carrots, string beans, cucumbers, potatoes, and all kinds of relishes, pickles, and hot rolls.

Later, desserts of mince pie, pumpkin pie, and gingerbread appeared on the table accompanied by tall mugs of cold cider.

When the dinner was over, Aunt Jenny nudged Uncle Andrew and whispered, "I reckon it's about time for Willie's next feeding. Perhaps we should leave now."

"Yes, we'll say our goodbyes to everyone and I'll bring the wagon 'round so we can be on our way."

And with that, they set off for home.

The Devereux Mansion

Rose's eyes widened at the sight of the mansion. It was an enormous two story red brick structure near the road, with a beautiful flower garden to the right of it.

Chapter 4
Erie Canal Outing

Sunday, August 16, 1840

We had a wonderful time at the mansion last night. It was an elegant place with French wallpaper on the walls of the large rooms. Tall carved mantels and shiny silver candelabras topped the huge fireplaces. The relatives even have a new invention called an icebox to keep food cold. It is a wooden box with a tin lining that holds ice in the top part and food in the middle. A pan below catches the water as the ice melts. A man delivers blocks of ice to the house to replace the ice that has melted. Aunt Jenny said she wants to get one some day.

The gardens have an assortment of beautiful flowers the likes of which I have never seen before. I do not even know the names of most of them.

The seven-course dinner was delicious. I had never eaten wild roast turkey before. It was quite good. I was so full, I did not reckon I would be able to eat dessert, but *when they brought out the pumpkin pie, I just had to have a bit of it.*

Uncle Andrew pointed out several other mansions in the area, on the way to the party. Mama was right. Utica is a beautiful city.

Maggie left as soon as we got home, but not before she made me promise I would tell her all about the festivities when I see her tomorrow.

I wonder how my family in Albany is doing. Surely, my little brother Caleb's leg is better by now. I miss them and my cousins on the boat. I especially miss talking to Charles, the hired hoggee.

Rose

"Rose," Uncle Andrew called, "it's time for church. Can you help get the boys ready? Aunt Jenny is staying home with Willie. The party really tired her out. I think it be better that she rest."

"I'll be right there," Rose called down. She put her journal away, grabbed a hat, and ran downstairs.

She helped Uncle Andrew give the boys their breakfast and made sure they were presentable. Then they all got into the wagon and went down the road to Saint John's Church.

"I'm so pleased you are here to help, Rose. It makes things much easier for Jenny," Uncle Andrew said.

Rose smiled and felt her face flush. "I'm happy to be able to lend a hand," she said, hoping Uncle Andrew did not notice her face.

The boys fidgeted on the way over, but once they were inside the wooden building, they sat quietly through the Mass. A stern look from Uncle Andrew stopped any misbehavior before it could come about. When they returned, Aunt Jenny was in the kitchen waiting for them. "I feel so much better now that I was able to get more rest, so I decided to prepare lunch. However, you are not to eat, Miss Rose. Maggie was here and wants you to go on a picnic with her on the bank of the Erie Canal."

"May I go?" Rose asked.

"Certainly. Today is the Sabbath," smiled Aunt Jenny. "Uncle Andrew still has to milk the cows and do other chores that can't wait, but you don't have to work today. Go and have a good time."

"Thank you. That sounds great. Now I can get a better look at the canal in Utica," beamed Rose.

"I packed a basket of food for you to take."

Just then, Maggie burst in the door. "Mama says we can't go alone," she griped. "We have to go with my brothers, so they can look after us."

"Your brothers?" Rose's stomach tightened, and she started to feel uneasy.

"Yes," said Maggie. "You're still going, aren't you?" she added when she saw the look on Rose's face.

Rose wanted to say no. She did not even know Maggie's brothers. She was hoping to have some good talks with Maggie on the picnic. Now the boys would spoil the whole thing. Yet, she did not want to disappoint her friend, so she reluctantly agreed to go.

"Samuel and Seth are waiting down by the road with our food basket," said Maggie. "Let's go. Oh, one more thing... I have to warn you about Seth. He likes to play jokes on people. So just ignore him if he bothers you."

Rose picked up her basket and followed Maggie down the path to the road. She did not think she was going to like this.

"Rose, this is my brother Samuel and this is Seth," Maggie announced when they reached the road. "Boys, this is my friend Rose. Now be nice to her," she added, looking directly at Seth.

Samuel, the taller of the two by four inches, had brown hair and eyes like Maggie. Seth was about as tall as Rose was, with blond hair that the summer sun had bleached almost white.

"Pleased to meet you," said Rose, feeling the heat rising in her face. Why did she always have to blush?

"Hello," said Samuel.

"*Very* pleased to meet you," said Seth as he bowed almost to the ground.

Rose's face turned beet red.

"Seth," scolded Maggie, "I told you to behave."

"Oh, all right," he said.

"Let's get going. I'm starved," said Samuel.

The girls walked up front, and the boys followed with the picnic baskets. They were silent for the first couple of blocks. Then Rose reckoned she could feel something tugging at her hair. She ignored it at first, and then she turned around to look. The boys were several steps behind them. It could not have been them. She must have been imagining things. As she turned forward, it started happening again. This time she turned quickly and caught Seth in the act.

"Stop it!" Rose yelled.

"Yes, stop. I'm going to tell Papa," Maggie warned.

"It was all in fun," Seth teased. "Don't you like to have fun, Rose?"

"Not that kind of fun," said Rose, thinking Seth was going to be just like her cousin Bridget, a bad egg. Rose was happy Samuel had been quiet the whole time. At least he seemed normal.

They walked a short distance further and were soon on the bank of the Grand Canal. There were many boats traveling in both directions. People sat on the roofs of the packets, admiring the view. The hoggees were walking the mules that hauled the boats. It was a hot summer day and the bright sun made the water glisten.

"Let's find a spot for the quilt so we can eat," said Samuel. By now, he was so hungry he could have eaten a horse.

"How about under those elms?" asked Maggie.

"That sounds good. We won't get too hot there," said Samuel.

They walked over to the elms, spread out the quilt, and sat down. Rose was just about to open her basket when

35

Seth pulled it away from her. She leaned forward to grab it, and Seth again pulled the basket away, causing her to fall flat on her face.

"Are you all right, Rose?" Maggie jumped up to help her friend.

Rose was more embarrassed by the fall than she was hurt by it. A tear rolled down her cheek and then another. She ran away from the group, so they would not see her cry. She hated Seth for doing that. He was so unpredictable; one might never know what else he would do. She wished she were home.

"Seth Evans, you are in a fix now!" Maggie shouted as she ran after her friend. "Rose, are you all right?" she said catching up to her.

"Yes. I'm just not used to someone who likes to joke so much," said Rose wiping her eyes with her dress, trying to calm down.

"Let's go back to the picnic," said Maggie. "I don't think Seth will start anymore trouble. He looked worried when you fell."

"I hope not."

When they reached the quilt, the boys were chowing down the food as fast as they could put it in their mouths.

"Are you okay?" Seth asked sheepishly.

"Yes," Rose said, glaring at him.

"Hey! Save some food for us!" yelled Maggie.

"There's plenty in these baskets. I reckon our mothers thought they were feeding a cavalry," said Samuel.

36

Rose loosened up a bit now that the cry had released some of her tension. She and Maggie fixed themselves plates of food and ate to their hearts' content. The chicken, cheese, apples, cold slaw, pickles, and cider tasted so good. After all that had happened, they were starved.

"Listen!" Seth jumped up. "Who has the guts to go swimming in the canal? How about it, Maggie? Samuel? Rose?"

"NO!" they all shouted at once.

"Come on. Who dares me to do it?"

"Not I," said Rose.

"I...dare...you!" said Samuel. He could not resist playing along with Seth even if it was against the law.

"No, Seth," shouted Maggie. "Don't do it. Please don't."

"You don't think I'll do it. Do you?" Seth said. "Come on Rose, I dare you to jump in with me." He grabbed Rose's arm and dragged her over to the edge of the towpath.

"No, no. Help me, someone," Rose shrieked trying to pull away from him.

"Let her go!" Samuel shouted as he rushed over to help her.

"I can't swim," she screamed.

Samuel freed her arm from Seth's grip. Rose began to tremble from head to toe and broke out in a cold sweat.

"Chicken!" Seth yelled as he jumped into the canal.

"You better sit down until you feel better," Samuel said to Rose. He did not reckon she would be so frightened. He felt sorry for her.

Seth swam out a little ways and then turned over on his back and floated. "Watch me," he shouted. "The water is great. Come on in!"

"Get back here," Maggie yelled. The boys always ruined everything when they were around.

"No, this is great," Seth hollered. "Very refreshing on a hot day."

"What if you get hit by a boat?" Rose called out, her voice still shaky.

"Won't happen!" Seth yelled.

"I'll go get him out," said Samuel as he started to walk towards the canal. He was always rescuing his brother.

As soon as he said that, they saw a police boat approach Seth and seize him. Two men put him on the deck, came over to the shore, and brought him up to where the others was standing.

"There is no swimming in the canal during the day, Seth Evans. You know that young man," the first police officer said.

"The fine for your actions today is two dollars. We'll be sure to collect it from your father," the other one added.

"Don't let this happen again," they warned as they got back in their boat and left.

"Papa is going to be mad as a March hare, Seth," Maggie said. "Two dollars is a lot of money. He could buy ten pounds of nails and four dinners in a restaurant for two dollars."

"I reckon we better head on home after this," said Samuel as he helped Rose up.

They packed up the quilt and their baskets and started up the street. Seth did not say much on the way home, knowing he was in big trouble.

This time, Rose and Maggie walked several steps behind her brothers. That way, the girls knew just where the boys were, and what they were doing.

"I'm so sorry Rose. I did not know this was going to happen. Seth can be rambunctious, but I've never seen him this bad," Maggie said in a low voice.

"It's not your fault," whispered Rose. She finally stopped trembling.

"Ah! I reckon he was showing off in front of you." Maggie finally figured it out.

"You reckon so?" Rose asked as her face turned bright pink.

Samuel
Evans

Seth
Evans

Chapter 5
Mail and Mischief

Monday, August 17, 1840

I had the most awful experience yesterday. Maggie's brother, Seth, is the most aggravating person in the world. He is even worse than Bridget is. I hope I never see the likes of him again.

Her other brother, Samuel, is entirely the opposite. He is kind and helpful and good looking, too, but quiet like me. It seems odd they could be brothers. They are so different.

Well, back to the dreadful happening of yesterday. Maggie decided we should go on a picnic on the bank of the Erie Canal. Her mother insisted that her brothers go with us to look after us. The minute we got on the road, Seth kept pulling my hair. When we got there, he kept teasing me by yanking the picnic basket away from me until I fell right on my face. Then he tried to pull me into the canal with him when he decided to go swimming in it. I was so scared I could not stop shaking for a long time. The police finally caught him and fined him. It was so embarrassing. He ruined the whole picnic for us. I never even got to talk to Maggie at all that day.

Maggie's Papa was very angry when he found out about the shenanigans Seth pulled and the two-dollar fine. He said he would pay the fine, but Seth would have to earn the money some how and pay him back. I do not know how he is going to earn that much money.

I had to get up early today to help Aunt Jenny with the breakfast. The men go out, work for a couple of hours, and then come in to eat. It seems like all they do is work and eat all day long.

I like working with Aunt Jenny because she tells me stories about her life and interesting things that happened in Utica in the past. I guess she takes after her brother, my Uncle Dermot, who is a great storyteller.

I better get down to the kitchen. It is time to start preparing lunch.

Rose

"Rose," said Aunt Jenny when she saw her, "there you are. Uncle Andrew had to go downtown for some nails and while he was there, he picked up the mail at the post office. There were two letters there for you. They were only eight cents each so he paid for them and brought them home." .

"Letters. For me? One is probably from my Mama, but I wonder who the other one could be from," said Rose.

"They're right on the kitchen table," said Aunt Jenny.

Rose picked one up and looked at the wax seal on the back. It had the letter S imbedded in the wax. "That one's from my Mama," she said excitedly as she broke the seal and unfolded the letter.

August 1840

Dear Rose,

We all miss you very much. We hope you had a good trip there on the canal and are enjoying the company of your aunt, uncle, and cousins. Caleb's leg is getting better. He wants to run around, so I have a difficult time keeping him off his feet. Papa won a prize for one of his articles in the paper. It was five dollars. We all went to a tavern for supper to celebrate and we bought some lottery tickets with the rest of the money.

We can't wait to get you home again.

Love and kisses,
Mama, Papa,
Cassie, Robert, and Caleb

The letter brought tears to her eyes and made her miss them even more.

"What about the other letter?" asked Aunt Jenny. "Who do you reckon that is from?"

Rose picked it up and turned it over. "I don't know. It doesn't have an initial on it," she said as she broke the seal and unfolded the letter. She glanced at the bottom signature. "Oh! It's from my cousin Bridget. I wonder what this is all about," Rose continued. She went into the hall to read the letter.

August 1840

Dear Rose,
How are you doin at Aunt Jenny and Uncle Andrew's farm? We are fine here on the boat. Sinse you were gone I have been talkin to Charles a hole lot more. I even help him with the mules some days. Me and him are very good frends now. One nite I showd him how to dance when we had a party on the boat. I mis you and can't wate to see you again.

Yor cuzin,
Bridget

"Oh no," Rose exclaimed as she walked into the kitchen with the letter.

"What is it?" Aunt Jenny said alarmed. "Is it bad news?"

"No. It is just that Bridget. She is so irritating. Now that I am not on the boat, she has been taking over my friendship with Charles. And she's doing things with him. And she taught him how to dance." Rose sounded frantic.

"Why, Rose Stewart, I do reckon you're jealous," said Aunt Jenny.

"No, I'm not!" Rose said too quickly while her heartbeat quickened, and she could feel the redness creep up her neck into her face.

"I hate that Bridget," she said, under her breath, as she ripped up the letter and ran up to her room. Then the tears came. She missed her family. She missed Charles and wished she could see him again. She wished Bridget had not sent her that letter.

"Rose, I need your help," Aunt Jenny's gentle voice called from the bottom of the stairs.

Rose decided she better pull herself together and stop acting foolish. She would be seeing Charles soon on the way back home. "I'm coming," she called out as she wiped her eyes, tried to put a smile on her face, and went back to the kitchen.

"I'm sorry I upset you," said Aunt Jenny, looking worried.

"That's all right. I probably am jealous. You were right. Charles and I were good friends on the boat, and now Bridget is trying to take my place with him."

Aunt Jenny laughed. "Bridget can be quite a handful. She always gets in trouble when the family is here for the winter. Even Maggie has a hard time getting along with her."

"If truth be told, it seems like Maggie could get along with just about anyone," said Rose.

"Why don't you take the boys outside for awhile? I already gave them their lunch, and I will tend to Uncle Andrew and Joe. Willie is sleeping right now so I have the time."

"Very well. Come on boys." Rose picked up George and took Benjamin by the hand while Jared lagged behind.

45

She reckoned it would be good for her to get out in the fresh air, so she could clear her mind. George and Benjamin went right to their usual dirt pile and began to build with rocks and sticks.

As Rose sat on the bottom of the porch steps, she noticed Jared, inching his way over to her.

"Mama is not going away, is she," he stated firmly.

"That's what I told you before," said Rose.

"You're just here to help her," Jared continued, assuring himself.

"Yes, and I'll be going home to my own family soon."

"You're not here to take my Mama's place."

"I would never, ever do that," said Rose.

"Then.... I love you," he said as he reached over and hugged her.

Rose felt her heart melt as she hugged him back. "I love you, too." She had finally won him over. "Now, go play with the boys."

"All right," he said as he ran over to the dirt pile.

Rose was still smiling, thinking about Jared's transformation when she saw Seth walking up the path from the road, whistling.

"Hello there, Miss Rose," he said as he approached her. Then he bowed from the waist.

"What are you doing here?" Rose sputtered, hoping it was all a bad dream. He was the last person she wanted to see.

"I'm here to paint one of your uncle's outbuildings. My father talked to your uncle who said I could earn two dollars for doing it."

"Do tell," said Rose. "You mean you didn't get punished more than that?"

"I wouldn't say that; my backside is still a little sore," he grimaced.

Rose was sorry she asked. It was more than she wanted to know.

"I need to tell your uncle that I have to do my own work first, so I won't be able to come over until after supper. I reckon it will take about three or four days to do the job."

"He's up in the field." Rose gestured towards the back of the house.

"All right," said Seth as he headed up that way.

Hmm, Rose thought, *maybe Seth has learned his lesson and will not act so foolish anymore.*

Rose became aware of something that felt like a pebble, hit her head. Could the wind blow that hard? Soon another and then another sailed over her head. Could it rain pebbles? She glanced upwards at the roof. Maybe they rolled off it.

The boys stopped playing, looked at Rose, and began to laugh. Soon they were pointing at her and giggling as hard as they could.

"What is wrong with me? Do I have a spider on me or something?" Just then, a dead mouse appeared before her eyes. She jumped up, screaming, "Help! Help!" as shivers ran up and down her spine. She kept shrieking, twisting, and trying to get out from under it.

Then she saw Seth. He was standing behind her making faces at the boys, holding a long stick in his hand with a dead mouse tied to the end of it.

"Seth!" she yelled at him. "How did you get back here? I thought you were up in the field talking to Uncle Andrew." Now she was angry that she had fallen for another of his tricks.

"I ran around the back of the house and here I was. I thought I'd have a little fun," he laughed. "I skeered you, didn't I?"

"Yes! And it's not funny, Seth." Rose tried to compose herself. "I wish you wouldn't play jokes on me."

"Why not? You are easy to skeer and you get so upset. It's fun to watch you. See you later." With that, he ran up into the field to talk to Uncle Andrew.

That reminded Rose of her resolution to follow Bridget's advice, *Do the thing that you're scared of, and the more you do it the less scared you'll be.* She hadn't been so good at following that advice lately. But Seth's tricks were unexpected, and she had no warning they were coming. Therefore, that advice wouldn't be a help. The only thing she could do was to try to ignore his silly behavior and pretend it did not bother her. That would not be easy to do.

"That Seth," said Rose, clenching her fists. "I'm going to have to think of a way to get even with him!"

Soon another figure was walking up the path. This time it was Samuel. "Hello, Rose," he said. "Is my brother here? Papa wants him to get back to work. He sent me after him."

"Yes, he's up in the field talking to my Uncle Andrew, but he had to cut a few shines on me first."

"Oh, that's why he's been gone so long. What did he do?"

"He dangled a dead mouse in front of my face and scared the living daylights out of me," complained Rose.

"I'm sorry. That is Seth for you. He always has to be the life of the party."

"And you, what do you do?" Rose surprised herself by asking.

"Oh, I just pick up the pieces after his mistakes," Samuel said, looking down at his feet.

Was that color Rose detected on his face? Why, he was just as timid as she was. "No, I mean what do you like to do?" she asked.

"Well, other than that, I like to swim, play checkers and marbles, fish, read, and I especially like politics. They are so interesting," he said, glancing up at her. His face reddened a little more.

"Then you must know a lot about what is going on in Utica."

"Yes. I am up on all of that. Do you like politics, too?" he asked excitedly as he finally looked her in the eye.

"No, but I like history and that's close," Rose said, smiling. "I'd like to talk to you about Utica some time."

49

"Sure, any time," Samuel said, looking down again.

Just then, another figure started up the path. It was Maggie and she looked irritated.

"There you are, Samuel. And where is Seth? Papa needs you both right away."

"Seth's up in the field," Samuel and Rose answered together. They looked at each other, smiled, and both looked away.

"Get home right now, Samuel. I'll go up into the field and get Seth. Sorry Rose, I can't stay but I'll see you later." Maggie hurried off to find her other brother.

Chapter 6
Seth Gets Tricked

Thursday, August 20, 1840

There has been so much going on here this week that I did not even get to my journal until today. Seth has been coming over in the evenings to paint the shed. Tomorrow he will finally be finished with it.

I managed to trick him on Tuesday. Before he came over, Maggie helped me dig a deep hole right next to the shed. We poured a lot of water into it to make it muddy. Then we put thin sticks over it both ways and covered it with leaves. We also scattered leaves and twigs all around the base of the shed, so you could not tell the hole was there.

I sat on the porch, and when Seth came up the path, I told him Uncle Andrew wanted him to start with the side the hole was on. He said, "Fine", put the paint in the pail, and started painting. As he moved to the right, he came closer and closer to the hole. With the next step he took, he *fell into the hole; the pail of paint fell in, too, and landed on his head. I laughed so hard I almost fell off the porch. Seth's feet were stuck in the mud and he had a hard time getting out. Paint dribbled down his face, over his clothes, and even into his muddy shoes. He yelled at me but could not say anything too much, after the shines he pulled on me the other day. He had to go straight home to change. Every time I think of him standing there full of paint, I start laughing all over again. Ha! Ha!*

We did not do anything to him yesterday, but he was very cautious as to where he stood when he was painting and tested the ground before he took a step.

Maggie is coming over later, and we are going to try to think of another way to trick him.

Rose

Rose dashed down the stairs and found Aunt Jenny in the kitchen, starting to make breakfast. "I'm here to help," she said.

"Good, I could use a hand," Aunt Jenny said. "The men will be in before too long. I already fed Willie and he went back to sleep. The boys are not up yet."

"Aunt Jenny, how did you meet Uncle Andrew and end up on the farm when Uncle Dermot is on the Canal, and Mama is in Albany?" asked Rose.

"You start cooking the ham, and I'll tell you while I prepare the eggs and toast," said Aunt Jenny.

52

"Do tell," said Rose.

"Well, my brother, Dermot, came here from Ireland in 1819 because there were too many people and no opportunities to make a living there. He heard there were jobs digging the canal that paid very well here. He went to work right away doing just that and saved every penny he made. In five years, he had enough money to send for us. He wanted our parents to come too, but they did not want to leave their homeland. Your mother and I came over on a huge boat, and when we got here, we had to find jobs because we did not have any money.

Dermot knew Uncle Andrew's parents and asked if they needed any help on the farm. Seeing as two of their daughters had married and moved out West to live, they said they could use some help in exchange for room and board. Therefore, Darcy and I moved in as servants. Your mother met your father while we were here, married him, and moved to Albany before the year was up. I stayed and worked on the farm.

Uncle Andrew took a shine to me and I liked him, but we had to keep our friendship a secret because his parents would not want him to marry a servant girl.

When the cholera sickness came in 1832, his parents got it first and died within a day of each other. Then all of the children came down with it. Uncle Andrew and I took care of them. And they died too, one by one. It was so heartbreaking." Aunt Jenny paused as she wiped her eyes with her apron.

"Then Uncle Andrew came down with the cholera. I was so afraid he was going to die, like the others. He barely hung on to life for a few days. I was spared even though I nursed him back to health. Finally, he started getting better and better. It took him a long while to get over the loss of almost his whole family, but eventually he did."

"That's what happened to Charles' family, too. He lost them to the cholera and became an orphan," said Rose.

"Is that your young man?" asked Aunt Jenny. "The one in Bridget's letter?"

"He's just a friend. Uncle Dermot hired him as a hoggee on the boat," Rose said, her face turning pink, "but tell me the rest of *your* story."

"Soon Uncle Andrew asked me to marry him and in a month we said our vows. He inherited the farm as the oldest son, and we ran it together with Joe who never got the cholera either."

"Oh, Aunt Jenny, that is so romantic!" sighed Rose.

"Hush up now. Here come the men," Aunt Jenny said. "And.... the boys," she added as Jared, Benjamin, and George ran down the stairs into the kitchen.

"You boys are just in time for breakfast," said Rose. "Sit down."

The men sat, ate quickly, and were back out in the field haying, while the boys dawdled.

"Jared, as soon as you are finished eating, I want you to go out and feed the chickens," said Aunt Jenny.

"Yes, Mama," he answered.

"I want to help, too," whined Benjamin.

"You can help, but don't let the chickens peck at you," said Aunt Jenny.

"Yes, Mama." Benjamin was in his glory as the two boys picked up the feed pail and went outside.

"Me, too?" asked George hopefully.

"No," said Aunt Jenny, "you're too little. You need to stay inside. You can watch us make butter."

George looked disappointed but did not complain. He sat down and started playing with an old pan.

"Rose, can you bring the churn here?" asked Aunt Jenny.

"Sure."

"I already skimmed the cream off the milk, soured it, and it is at the right temperature," said Aunt Jenny. "Now all we have to do is pour it into the churn and keep plunging it until it separates into buttermilk and butter."

"That sounds easy," said Rose as she followed Aunt Jenny's directions and started plunging and plunging and plunging.

In the meantime, Aunt Jenny fed Willie, changed his diaper, and put both him and George upstairs for a nap. When she came downstairs, Rose was still plunging.

"How long does this take?" Rose asked. "My arms are getting tired."

"It takes about an hour; you should be almost done," laughed Aunt Jenny. "Let me take a look at it."

"Sure," said Rose glad to be able to take a break.

"It's butter!" Aunt Jenny announced. "Now we need to pour out the buttermilk and wash the butter with water until there is no more milk in it."

"I can do that," said Rose, taking hold of the butter after Aunt Jenny poured the buttermilk into a large container.

"Good. It takes about three or four washings to get it right," instructed Aunt Jenny.

Rose washed the butter and placed it on the table.

"Now, we must add salt to it to preserve it." Aunt Jenny got an earthenware container from the shelf while Rose worked the salt into the butter.

"You can form the butter into a ball and put it in the container, and we are finished," said Aunt Jenny.

"What are you going to do with the buttermilk?" Rose was curious.

"We'll have it for supper. It's delicious as a drink," said Aunt Jenny.

"Where do you keep the butter?" asked Rose.

"Can you bring it down to the cold part of the cellar where the other things are stored?" asked Aunt Jenny.

"Sure," said Rose.

When she came upstairs, she found Maggie waiting for her.

"Why don't you girls take a break and go out on the porch? In about an hour, it will be time to start supper. I'll call you then, Rose."

"Did you think of another way to trick Seth?" asked Rose when they were outside.

"I didn't have too much time to think, so I reckon we could do that together right now," said Maggie as she sat down next to Rose on the porch steps.

"We could give him a drink with a lot of salt in it," said Rose.

"It would only take Seth one sip to notice that," said Maggie.

"Do you have any other ideas?" asked Rose.

"We can't do the hole thing again," said Maggie.

"No. But wait a minute…I have the perfect idea," said Rose. "Let's put a pail of water over the door of the shed and tie it to the handle of the door. When Seth opens the door to get the paint, the pail will tip and the water will spill on him."

"That's a great idea," said Maggie.

"Let's do it," said Rose.

They scrambled off the porch and set up the plan. Then Maggie went home, and Rose went in to help Aunt Jenny with the supper. She chuckled every time she thought of what would happen to Seth later.

After supper, Maggie hurried back to see Rose. They hid behind one of the tall, thick bushes and waited.

Soon Seth came whistling up the path. Tonight he would finish painting, and he would have his two dollars to pay back Papa. He walked over to the shed to get the paint, pulled the door open and stepped inside. Not only did the water fall on him like the girls had planned, but the pail fell down and hit him in the head. He screamed and then fell silently to the floor. A bump started rising on his forehead.

57

Maggie and Rose laughed and laughed, but when Seth did not get up, they stopped and came out from behind the bush. They ran over to him and stood looking at him. His eyes were closed, and he was not moving.

"Seth!" Maggie called.

No answer.

Rose was beginning to panic. "Seth, get up!" she yelled.

He did not move.

"What if we killed him?" Rose was starting to shake all over.

"We better get your uncle," said Maggie.

Just then, Aunt Jenny appeared at the door. "What's going on out here? I thought you were…What happened to Seth?" she gasped when she saw him lying on the shed floor.

"Aunt Jenny, Aunt Jenny, we tried to play a joke on Seth, and we might have killed him!" yelled Rose.

"Nonsense. But you might have knocked him out," she said when she saw the pail next to him. "Is he breathing?"

The girls inched closer to him and bent down to check.

Seth jumped up, laughing wildly, pushing them aside. "Gotcha," he said. "Now who got tricked?"

The girls went weak in the knees and almost dropped to the floor.

Aunt Jenny just laughed. "Maybe you girls better not try to trick the master trickster," she said. "Now you're both going to have to help Seth finish painting since your trick made him loose valuable time."

Chapter 7
An Interesting Chat

Saturday, August 22, 1840

Maggie and I tricked Seth when he came over to paint yesterday, but the trick backfired on us. I have learned my lesson about playing tricks. I will never do that again! Someone could get hurt bad for real. Even Maggie was frightened about what happened. I do not know how Seth can pull shines over and over and not be bothered by the consequences. We had to help Seth finish painting the shed as a punishment.

Aunt Jenny seems to be getting stronger by the day and will not need my help soon. She has changed so much since I got here. However, I reckon she was just exhausted then.

I will be leaving for home in one more week. I cannot wait to see my Mama, Papa, Cassie, Robert, and Caleb. It will be good to be able to sleep in my own bed again. I wonder if Caleb's leg healed and if he is able to walk yet. I hope so. I am not anxious to see Bridget, though. I am

59

going to give her a piece of my mind about that letter she wrote me.

Today Maggie is coming over to show me how to quilt. She said it is a good way to use up small bits of cloth left over from sewing. I have done needlework before, but I have never made a quilt. I am ready to learn.

Rose

Rose helped Aunt Jenny prepare breakfast, served the men and boys, cleaned up the kitchen, dressed the boys, and went out on the porch to wait for Maggie. She had a box of scrap cloth, thread, and a needle that Aunt Jenny fixed for her.

The boys fed the chickens and were now playing in their usual dirt pile. Jared seemed to be in charge; he was having Benjamin look for sticks and leaves. George's job was to collect stones.

Finally, Maggie was coming up the path. Oh no, it was not Maggie. It was Samuel. What was he doing here?

"Good morning, Rose," he said shyly.

"Hello Samuel. Where's Maggie?"

"Mama sent me over here to tell you that Maggie had a stomach ache." He glanced at her and then away. "And she can't come over now." He seemed uneasy. "But if she feels better this afternoon, she will be here later," he added.

Rose wondered if that was how she looked when she was anxious.

Samuel turned to go.

"Samuel, wait a minute." Now she felt bold for a change. "Remember the last time we talked, and you said you knew a lot about Utica and you liked politics."

"Yes." His whole being came alive when she mentioned the word politics. He turned back to face her. "Papa lets me sit in on the meetings he and his friends have at the house."

"What kind of meetings?" asked Rose.

"Oh, just get-togethers where they talk about the city and what's happening here. It's very interesting."

"Do tell," said Rose.

"Someday when I get older, I want to be an alderman on the common council. Maybe I can even become mayor some day. I think Utica is a grand city, and I want to help it become even better. I also want to lend a hand to the people here."

He sounded so energized it gave Rose goose bumps. She had never heard Samuel talk so much. "You certainly would make an excellent mayor. You are very thoughtful and kind," she said.

Samuel's face turned crimson. "It's nice of you to say so," he said, trying to cover his face with his hands.

Rose was surprised to see a boy go red in the face. "Samuel, do you know I have the same problem. I seem to blush at the drop of a hat," she said.

"You do? I never would have thought that. You seem so sure of yourself." He began to relax a little.

Rose laughed when he said that. "I'm starting to get over it since I have been to so many new places and met so many new people lately."

"Do you think I'll get over it, too?"

"You will as soon as you start making those speeches when you get into politics," Rose said.

"That's the one thing that bothers me. I know I'll have to give speeches and I hope I can do it."

"You will! Let me pass on some advice my cousin on the boat gave me. She said, 'Just do the thing you're scared of, and the more you do it the less scared you'll be.' It works. I have been trying to live by it and it has helped."

"That sounds good. I reckon I'll try that," Samuel said. "Maybe I can practice making speeches."

"Just tell everyone what you just told me. Speak from your heart and no one will be able to resist voting for you."

"Thank you, Rose. You are a great girl. I'm so happy to have met you." His voice was full of life again.

That made Rose blush. "See," she said pointing to her face.

They both laughed at that.

"What do you want to do when you get older?" Samuel asked.

"I want to be a writer like my Papa. He works for the newspaper in Albany," Rose said. "I know women don't have the same rights as men, but there are some women writers like Jane Austin and Dorothea Dix, and I hope to follow in their footsteps."

"You are right. Women can't even vote, they can't serve on juries, and if they work, they only get half the pay men do."

"It's not fair," said Rose.

"At least women have more rights than the slaves," said Samuel.

"That's true. But I thought slavery was abolished in York State."

"It was, but not in the South. Many people here oppose slavery and are trying to help slaves escape to freedom in Canada."

"Do tell," Rose was in awe of what Samuel was saying.

"Have you ever heard of the Underground Railroad?" Samuel asked. "Wait maybe I'm boring you with all this talk."

"Oh, no. I find it fascinating. Do tell."

"The Underground Railroad is a series of hiding places called stations where slaves can stay safely, on their way from the South to freedom. The stations are in schools, churches, stores, or even people's houses. The slaves move during the night when it is dark, so they will not be seen. John De Long's house on John Street is a station. He always leaves his door open, and many times in the morning, he will find slaves sleeping on the floor. He gives them food and clothes. And then his son, Mark, takes them to North Utica and from there up North through Deerfield to escape."

"Are there other stations in Utica?" Rose hung on to Samuel's every word.

"They say William Blaikie, the pharmacist on Genesee Street, provides a station, and Joshua Howe's cabin between the end of Utica and the beginning of New Hartford is one, as well as the Bleecker Street Methodist Church," said Samuel, looking around to make sure no one else was listening.

"You sure do know a lot about Utica," said Rose.

Maggie marched up the path shouting, "Samuel, Papa is looking for you. You have been here for almost two hours. He needs your help right now!"

"Sorry, Rose, I have to go. Bye," Samuel said as he turned and hurriedly headed for home.

"Bye," said Rose.

"I feel better now, so I'm here to show you how to quilt," Maggie said. "Was my brother talking to you all that time?" she asked.

"Yes," said Rose starting to blush.

"He hardly ever says more than two words to anyone."

"Really?" said Rose. "He told me all about his wish to get into politics and work to help the people of the city. He is so ambitious."

"He told you all that. My brother?" asked Maggie.

"We talked about a whole lot of other things too," said Rose.

"He must like you then." Maggie smiled. Now she understood why Samuel was gone so long.

Rose's face turned crimson, and her heart pounded like a drum. "I thought you were going to show me how to

64

quilt," she said, changing the subject as quickly as possible.

"That's right. Did you get the scraps of cloth, thread, and needle?"

"Yes, Aunt Jenny put them in a box for me. She also gave me a pair of scissors, a ruler, and a pencil."

"Good. That's just what we will need," said Maggie. "First, you cut a whole lot of squares the same size." Maggie used the ruler to measure the scraps. Then she drew lines with the pencil to make a square. "I'll draw them and you can cut them out."

When they had several squares ready, Maggie took two of them, put right sides together, and showed Rose how to sew them together on one side. "You just keep adding squares to the piece the same way until you have about ten in a row."

"I can do that," said Rose. "How many of these rows do you make?" she asked.

"It depends on how long you want the quilt to be," said Maggie. "You can make some rows in your spare time, and the next time I come over I'll show you how to put them together."

"Great!" said Rose.

"I had better get on home, now. Mama will need help with lunch for the crew."

"Oh, my goodness, so will Aunt Jenny," said Rose. "I've been out here all morning." She quickly gathered up her quilting supplies and went inside.

Chapter 8
The Quilting Bee

Wednesday, August 26, 1840

I have been sewing my squares together in between my chores. I think I have enough rows to make a small quilt for little Willie. I am going to surprise Aunt Jenny with it when I leave. Maggie said she would help me finish it.

I had a great talk with Maggie's brother, Samuel, a few days ago. He is a very smart boy with a lot of ambition. Not many fifteen-year-olds would have the goals he has. Maybe he could be President of the United States some day. He is also ~~good looking~~ quite handsome.

Maggie has not been over since the day she showed me how to quilt. Her mother was not feeling well, so Maggie had a lot of extra work to do at her own house. She will be coming over tomorrow for Aunt Jenny's quilting bee.

Aunt Jenny said she better have the bee before I leave, or she would never have time for it when she was on her own. That means I need to help her get ready for it today.

We have to make several cakes and pies for the women to eat when they are finished with the quilt. It is up to the hostess to feed them, as they will be here most of the day.

I have never seen Aunt Jenny so excited, except for the time we went to the frolic at the mansion. She cannot wait to see her neighborhood friends again. She sent Uncle Andrew to all of their houses to inform them of the bee. Aunt Jenny said neighbors do not see much of each other unless they have these bees, because there is so much work to do on the farms.

I must go and get started helping Aunt Jenny bake.

Rose

"What would you like me to do, Aunt Jenny?" asked Rose as she went into the kitchen.

"You can start peeling the apples for the pies. I'm making the crusts now." She had several pie tins lined up on the table and was mixing the ingredients for the dough in a large wooden bowl.

Rose put on her apron and began the job.

"We'll bake the pies first and make the cakes after supper. Benjamin, George, and Willie are up for a nap and Jared is playing outside in the dirt pile," said Aunt Jenny, sounding like a bubble about to burst. "Uncle Andrew will have to set the quilt rack up in the parlor. But first, he will have to move the furniture back. This is going to be such a treat!" Aunt Jenny could not stop talking.

"Do you ever have any other kind of bees?" asked Rose.

"Yes, lots of them. Too bad you will not be here in October. That's when we have our husking bees."

"What's a husking bee?" asked Rose mystified.

"It's when all the neighbors for miles around get together to husk their corn. Each neighbor has a turn to hold a husking bee. That way we all help each other to get the job done. After the husking, we have treats and cider and a great time talking and catching up on the news."

"That sounds like fun," said Rose. "Do tell. How does it take place?"

"The bee usually starts at seven in the evening. Several wagonloads of corn with husks are already in the barn in a huge pile. The boys and men do the husking while the women and girls sit around the edge of the barn on chairs, visiting. If a boy finds a red ear of corn, he can pick a girl to kiss. She can't refuse," said Aunt Jenny.

"I don't know if I'd like that," said Rose.

"Yes, you would. It's all in fun," said Aunt Jenny. "Sometimes the boys hide a red ear of corn in the lining of their jackets and pull it out during the husking, pretending they found it, if they especially want to kiss a certain girl."

"Do tell," said Rose. "And they don't get caught?"

"As I said before, it's all in fun. Uncle Andrew's parents had a husking bee the year I came to work for them. He hid a red ear of corn in the lining of his jacket and pulled it out during the husking, pretending he found it. Then he picked me to kiss. I was so embarrassed, but I had to let him.

A little later, he really found a red one in the pile he was husking, and he picked me again. Everyone's eyes were on us. My face turned beet red and after he kissed me, I ran off to the house to get the desserts ready." Aunt Jenny laughed. "I wasn't about to put up with any more of that nonsense."

Rose laughed, too.

They completed the pies and had them baking when Uncle Andrew came in. "Do you want me to set the quilt frame up for you in the parlor?"

"Yes, that would be good. Put it right in the middle of the room. You might have to move the furniture back some," Aunt Jenny instructed.

Just then, Willie started crying, and Aunt Jenny went up to feed him. Jared came in from outside and insisted he wanted to help put the quilt frame up. Uncle Andrew let him do it.

Rose decided she better start getting supper ready. She went into the kitchen and began cooking.

After supper, Rose and Aunt Jenny made the batter for a number of cakes, half chocolate and half vanilla. While the cakes were baking, Aunt Jenny and Rose went into the parlor to set the quilt up in the frame.

"This is a quilt top I just finished. It's called the Irish Chain pattern," said Aunt Jenny. She carefully unfolded it on the floor.

"Oh, Aunt Jenny, it's so beautiful," said Rose, fingering the pretty material.

They made three layers: a backing on the bottom, a filling of an old blanket in the middle that would make it nice and warm, and the pieced quiltop over all. It looked like a huge sandwich. Then they stretched and pinned it onto the frame, not too tight and not too loose.

"There. Now it is all ready for the women to quilt when they get here tomorrow morning," said Aunt Jenny.

"Do you need some chairs?" asked Rose.

"Yes," said Aunt Jenny. "Can you help get some from the other rooms? We need to put some all along the sides of the frame, so the women can sit there while they quilt."

"How many people do you think will come?" asked Rose.

"A whole lot. Be prepared. There will be younger women, older women, and many, many children. Most women know how to quilt, and the others know how to sew, so with a little guidance, they should be able to quilt too. Perhaps you and Maggie can help care for the children," said Aunt Jenny.

"But I wanted to try quilting, too," said Rose.

"You can. All the girls can take turns quilting and watching the children."

"Good," said Rose.

"Now, I reckon we better check on the cakes," said Aunt Jenny.

The cakes were done, and soon cool and frosted. "There. We're finished," said Aunt Jenny. "Time for bed."

70

Aunt Jenny's
Irish Chain Quilt

"Oh, Aunt Jenny, it's so beautiful," said Rose,
fingering the pretty material.

"Wa-a-a-a." A cry came from upstairs.

"Spoke too soon. *You* are finished. I still have to feed Willie," sighed Aunt Jenny.

Chapter 9
A Delightful Evening

Thursday, August 27, 1840

Aunt Jenny was up early this morning and full of energy. I reckon it was because of the bee yesterday. Right after breakfast, she decided to wash a huge batch of clothes and hang them outside to dry. There were so many things, it took three long clotheslines to fit them all. I helped and we were done in two hours. Now finally I escaped up here to write in my journal.

The quilting bee was spectacular. There were about twenty women and just as many children there. I was able to meet Maggie's mother, at last, who is a lot like her, friendly and fun to talk to.

Seth interfered again and caused a commotion at the quilting bee. He snuck over to our house and hid under the quilt frame. When all the women were seated around it, getting ready to quilt, he jumped up and lifted the quilt frame up into the air with his head. The women all screamed, had conniption fits, and one actually fainted. They were so scared until Seth popped his head out from under it. Then they scolded him. He thought it was hilarious and just kept laughing and laughing. He is crazy as a loon. His mother hollered at him, told him to go home, and said she would deal with him later. I hope she punished him good.

Maggie, I, and another girl named Sarah watched the children most of the time, but we did get to quilt. My stitches were too big at first but as I kept sewing, they kept getting smaller and smaller. Maggie was better at it than I was. I reckon she has been to many quilting bees.

When it was done, the quilt was so handsome with all the quilting designs the women used. Afterwards, we had the greatest time sharing news and stories and eating to our hearts' content.

The younger children had fun too, playing in the dirt pile and up in the field. Everyone was sorry when it was time to go home, but all said they looked forward to the next bee.

Maggie and her mother stayed to help us clean up when everyone had gone home.

I called Maggie up to my room and showed her the rows of squares I had sewn. She explained how to stitch them together into a quilt top. Maggie said you could tie a quilt as well as quilting one, and that was what we were going to do with mine because it was a lot faster. You just knot little pieces of cord that you pull through all three layers with a big needle where each square meets, and it is ready. I cannot wait to get it done and give it to Aunt Jenny for Willie.

Just four more days and I will be traveling home to Albany. I am so excited to know I will see my family soon. I am going to miss Aunt Jenny, Uncle Andrew, and the boys. Most of all, I will miss Maggie and Samuel. I will not miss Seth. No way, no how!!!

Rose

Aunt Jenny was singing as she prepared lunch when Rose came downstairs again.

"You sure had a good time yesterday, didn't you?" said Rose.

"It was wonderful, seeing all of my friends again."

"Do you need any help?"

"Not really. I'm almost done."

The men and boys came in, ate lunch quickly, and were back outside working.

After lunch, Aunt Jenny was tired, so she went up to nap with Willie, George, and Benjamin, leaving Rose in charge of Jared.

Rose decided to work on her quilt while she looked out the window occasionally to see what Jared was doing. The last time she looked, she saw the sky getting cloudy and dark. It kept getting even darker. Then she saw lightning flash across the sky and heard thunder rumbling in the distance. All she could think of was the time when she was on the boat and trapped outside on the deck, in a violent storm. The memory gave her the shivers.

Suddenly there was pounding and shouting at the door. "Rose, Rose, let us in!" It was Maggie, Samuel, and Seth along with Jared who fled the minute he saw the lightning.

"Mama saw your clothes on the line and sent us over to help you get them off before the rain comes," said Maggie.

"Hurry," said Samuel, "it could start any minute."

"It's going to be a bad one," said Seth. "Look at the sky. It is getting darker every minute."

They each grabbed a basket and ran towards the clotheslines, picking off the clothes as fast as they could. Jared stayed behind, covering his ears with his hands as he hid his face in the couch.

Lightning flashed, cutting the sky in half, followed by thunder so loud, they had to cover their ears. They ran with all their might to the house with Uncle Andrew and Joe not far behind.

"I guess we won't be getting any more work done today," said Uncle Andrew, "and you children are going to have to stay here until the storm is over."

"Mama said we could if it started before we were done," said Maggie.

The storm woke Aunt Jenny, and she came downstairs with the boys clinging to her, trying to hide behind her skirt. "My goodness, the weather sure did change fast. This morning the sun was shining brightly and now look at this," she said. "And my clothes are on the line," she shouted as she ran towards the door.

"We brought them in, Aunt Jenny," the foursome said at once.

"Bless you. At least my washing was not for nothing," said Aunt Jenny.

Then the rain started. It rained so hard it looked like it could last the 40 days it did in the Bible.

"What shall we do now that we can't do any work?" asked Uncle Andrew.

"I know," said Aunt Jenny. "Let's go into the parlor, light a whole lot of candles, and tell stories."

"Yes," said Rose. "That sounds great! And more stories about Utica. Do tell!"

"Would you believe that in the year 1802 Utica was just a crossroads with Bagg's Square at the center and a dozen houses and shops surrounding it? You'd never know that, with the size of it today," Uncle Andrew began.

"A dreadful thing happened six years ago this August," he continued. "A vicious cyclone hit Utica, blowing roofs off houses on Court Street, the spire off the Presbyterian Church on Bleecker Street, and downed the town clock."

"Wow, that must have been some storm," said Rose. "Tell us more!"

Just as she finished saying that, lightning burst across the sky again, lighting up the whole room, and loud claps of thunder followed immediately. Rose jumped in her seat and put her hands over her ears. She moved a little closer to Aunt Jenny on the couch.

"More Utica stories, let me see," said Uncle Andrew, thinking.

"In July of 1825 the famous General La Fayette visited Utica. He was taking a tour of the state in a canal boat. He got off the boat in Whitesboro and rode in a coach with a company of cavalry in front and behind him. The citizens decorated the city and fired off cannons. A luncheon and reception was held for him at Bagg's Hotel. Later he went to see the niece of President Adams, Mrs. Johnson. When he left the area on the canal boat, children threw flowers at him from the canal bridge at Third Street. Crowds of people lined the banks of the canal and cheered until the boat was out of sight. By the way, the street he traveled over was renamed Lafayette Street in his honor," Uncle Andrew concluded.

"That is so interesting!" said Rose.

"Samuel can tell the next one," said Uncle Andrew.

"Well, let's see. Four years ago, the Oneida Bank of Utica was getting ready for their grand opening. The night before the event, some thieves dared to break in and steal $116,500. in cash. It was a quarter of the banks assets. I can actually remember when it happened," said Samuel.

"That's a lot of money," said Maggie.

"One of the robbers was caught, but they never recovered all of the money," said Uncle Andrew.

"Oh my goodness, how awful," said Rose.

"Enough stories," said Aunt Jenny. "Why don't we roll back the rug and dance while we're waiting for the rain to stop. Joe can play his fiddle and we can all try that new dance, the polka."

"Sounds good to me," said Maggie.

"All right, everyone choose a partner," said Aunt Jenny. "I'll take Samuel."

"I'll take Uncle Andrew," Rose said quickly, so she would not be stuck with Seth. She was not even sure she knew how to do the dance right.

Maggie took Seth, and the three little boys danced in a group.

Joe started playing the fiddle, and the couples went whirling around the parlor floor.

"I'm not sure I can do this right," Rose said to Uncle Andrew. The palms of her hands were sweaty, and she was starting to feel uneasy.

"Don't worry. Just do what I do and have fun," said Uncle Andrew.

After a couple of false starts, stepping on Uncle Andrew's feet, Rose started to get the hang of it. Round and round they went.

"This actually is fun," Rose remarked as they whirled around again.

"Everyone change partners for the next one." Aunt Jenny sounded like she was reliving her childhood.

Rose ended up with Seth this time. Dancing with him was like dancing with a jumping jack. He kept stepping on her toes and hopping all around.

"Rose, I'm sorry I tortured you so much when you were here," Seth said as they bobbed along. That was something she never thought she would hear *him* say.

"Me, too!" Rose said. If he could say it, she could say it too.

"Switch partners again," called out Aunt Jenny.

This time Rose got Samuel. Their faces were both red now from the dancing, so neither could tell if the other were blushing. He was light on his feet, and she felt like she was flying when she danced with him.

"Where did you learn to dance like that?" asked Rose as they circled around the floor. "You are an excellent dancer!"

"My sister Maggie talks me into letting her practice with me," he said, hoping he didn't sound like a pushover.

After a few more partners and rounds, Aunt Jenny decided they all needed to rest, have some cold cider, and cool off.

When the rain finally stopped, Maggie and her brothers decided they had better go home. Joe left, too.

"Oh, Aunt Jenny, that was so much fun," said Rose.

"It was, wasn't it?"

"And Samuel is such a good dancer."

"He is, isn't he? What's more, he is as smart as a steel trap. And quite handsome, too," Aunt Jenny stated looking at Rose.

"That he is!" Rose said, blushing again. "Goodnight."

Chapter 10
Saying Good-Bye

Monday, August 31, 1840

I have been working hard on my quilt for Willie and have not had the time to write. I finally finished it. Maggie helped me put the binding on it.

Uncle Dermot should be arriving sometime today. I am both happy and sad; happy that I will be going home, but sad to leave Utica and my new friends and family here.

This trip has been the most wonderful experience I have ever had. I reckon I have traveled farther and seen more sights than the average Yorker. I learned so many new things, traveled on the Grand Canal, and visited many interesting places in Utica. What's more, I reckon I am starting to get over my shyness a little, but I would not say that I am bold.

I packed most of my things in my carpetbag last night. I just have to put in my journal and writing utensils. This will be my last entry until I get on the boat.

Rose

"Aunt Jenny, may I go over to Maggie's to say goodbye to her?" Rose asked.

"Certainly," said Aunt Jenny.

Rose half walked and half ran down the path and over the road until she was at Maggie's house. She had to wipe the tears that kept filling her eyes, so she could see where she was going. This was not going to be easy.

Rose was just about to knock at the door when Maggie opened it. "I was just coming over to your house," she said, "and here you are."

"I'm here to say goodbye. I'll be leaving sometime today," Rose could not look her in the eye.

"Oh, Rose," Maggie grabbed her by the shoulders, "I'm going to miss you so much," she cried and then hugged her.

"I'm going to miss you, too," said Rose, with the tears now streaming down her cheeks. "You have been such a good friend the whole time I was here."

"We can write, and maybe you can visit your Uncle Andrew and Aunt Jenny again," Maggie said hopefully. By now, tears filled her eyes and ran down her face.

"That would be grand," said Rose. "We can write, but I'm not so sure I will come to Utica again."

"Well then, maybe I'll come and visit you in Albany," said Maggie surprised at her own good idea.

"Would you? Could you?" asked Rose as she wiped her eyes. That made her feel somewhat better. She could not bear the idea of never seeing Maggie again.

"You bet!" Maggie wiped her eyes and gave Rose another hug. "Have a great trip home," she added.

Rose left the house, still feeling sad and teary eyed as she walked down the path. When she approached the road, Samuel stepped out from behind a bush.

Rose jumped. "Oh, you scared me! I thought you were a bear."

"I'm sorry. I did not mean to frighten you. I just wanted to say good-bye, and ask you something before you leave," said Samuel, his face turning color as he walked down the road beside her towards her aunt and uncle's house.

"What is it?" asked Rose, wiping the last of the tears from her eyes.

"Well..." he stammered, "we have had such great times talking, and we like many of the same things. I was wondering if..." he hesitated, loosing his nerve.

"If what?" asked Rose, wondering what he was trying to say.

"I was wondering...if I could write to you when you get back to Albany," he said all in one breath before he lost his nerve again.

"Sure," she said. "That would be fine. I reckon I would enjoy that. You could tell me all the news of Utica."

"Yes," he said, breathing a sigh of relief, feeling great that he had done the thing he feared, "and you can tell me all about Albany," he added.

"Well, I reckon this is good-bye then," Rose said as she stopped at the path to the farm.

"Good bye. I will miss you, Rose. You are a great girl," Samuel said as he stopped there as well. "So long," he added and turned to go back home. He looked back for a moment, waving and added, "Don't forget to look for a letter from me."

Rose would miss Samuel, too. He had shared a lot about his ambitions and his city with her. She smiled, remembering how surprised she was to see him blush when he first talked to her.

Rose walked slowly up the path. This was going to be a long, difficult day, having to say good-bye to everyone. She went into the house, ran upstairs, retrieved the quilt she made for Willie from under the bed, and went downstairs with it behind her back. She was in such a hurry, she almost ran into Aunt Jenny at the bottom of the stairs.

"Whoa, slow down, Rose." Aunt Jenny put her hands on Rose's shoulders.

"I have something for you. A going away present," Rose said, pulling the quilt out from behind her back. "Well actually, it's for Willie."

Aunt Jenny laughed.

"Don't you like it?" Tears filled Rose's eyes again.

"Sorry. I didn't mean to laugh. I love it! It's just that I have something for you too. Go see. It's on the dining room table." Aunt Jenny was also starting to feel weepy now.

Rose walked into the dining room. She could hardly believe what she saw. There sat the quilt the women had quilted at the quilting bee.

"Oh, Aunt Jenny, it… it's spectacular! Are you sure you want me to have it? You put so much work into it. It could keep you mighty warm this winter," Rose said.

"Of course I do," said Aunt Jenny. "You did so much work the whole time you were here, I wish I could give you more." Aunt Jenny hugged her and added, "I am going to miss you so much, Rose Stewart." Her voice trembled and her eyes watered.

"Why do good-byes have to be so hard?" asked Rose. Now they were both crying on each other's shoulders.

"What is the matter? Did someone get hurt?" Uncle Andrew asked when he came inside and saw them crying.

"No, we are just saying good-bye," they said at the same time, and then they both laughed.

"That's right. Today is the day Uncle Dermot is supposed to get here," said Uncle Andrew. "Well, Rose, thank you for helping Jenny with the baby and taking care of the boys. It was so nice to meet my niece at last. We are going to miss you," he added, giving her a hug.

"I'm going to miss all of you, too." The tears started again.

"Rose, Rose," Jared ran up to her shouting, "are you leaving today?"

"Yes. Remember I told you I would be going home," Rose said.

"I don't want you to go. You have to stay here," he pleaded.

Rose knelt down so she could look him in the eye. "I have to go. My Mama, Papa, brothers, and sister are waiting for me to come back home."

"But I want you here so you can tell us stories, and I love you," he whimpered and hugged her so hard it almost took her breath away. He thought if he held on to her tight enough, she might not go.

"I know you do, and I would love to stay, but I have to go home."

"All right…you can go," he said sadly.

Benjamin and George came running in looking for Jared.

"Rose is going home today, boys. Do you want to say good-bye?" Aunt Jenny asked.

"Goodbye, Rose," said Benjamin.

"Bye-bye," said George.

"Come here, you two. Give me a hug," said Rose ruffling their hair, reaching down to their height to embrace them.

They hugged her back and, along with Jared, went back out to their dirt pile.

"Anybody home," bellowed a deep voice from the back door.

"Uncle Dermot," yelled Rose as she ran to the door and gave him a big bear hug. "You're here."

"I'm here, all right, and Aunt Cora, Tom, Bridget, and Sean are right behind me. Came to see the baby, and then we are going to take you home to Albany, Rose." It was good to hear his booming voice again.

"Rose," yelled Bridget. "It's so good to see you." She ran over to hug Rose almost knocking her down. Rose stiffened as Bridget came towards her, remembering the letter she had written to her about Charles. She did not know if she could continue their friendship now, as it was when she left the boat.

Little Sean was right behind Bridget with another hug. "Do you still have the rock I gave you on the boat?"

"I sure do. It's packed away with my things now, but when I get home, I'm going to make a special place for it on my dresser."

Sean smiled when she said that and hugged her even harder. "I'm glad you're coming back with us. I missed you," he said.

"Where is Charles?" With all the commotion, Rose just realized that he was not with them.

"He knew this was just family, so he stayed to keep an eye on the boat," said Aunt Cora. "But I think he really wanted to catch up on his sleep. Did you have a good time, child?"

"Oh, it was wonderful," said Rose, forgetting about Bridget for the moment.

"Now, where's that baby? We want to see him," Uncle Dermot bellowed.

"He's upstairs. Do you want to get him, Rose?" asked Aunt Jenny.

"Yes, I'd love to." Rose tiptoed quietly up to Aunt Jenny's room and lifted Willie out of his crib.

He smiled and gooed when he saw her.

"Sweet Willie. I am going to miss you all to pieces when I go home. All to pieces!" She almost cried again as she kissed the top of his head. "But now you are going to meet your other cousins," she said as she carried him down the stairs.

"There's that big boy!" boomed Uncle Dermot.

"What a darling!" said Aunt Cora.

"Can I hold him?" asked Bridget.

Rose glanced at Aunt Jenny, who nodded, and she gave the baby to Bridget. "Make sure you hold his head up," she said to her cousin.

Bridget held him for a while and passed him on to Uncle Dermot who in turn gave him to Aunt Cora.

"Bridget, I need to talk to you outside for a minute," said Rose, heading towards the door.

"Sure," said Bridget and followed her outside.

"What's been going on between you and Charles?" grumbled Rose.

"What do you mean?" asked Bridget, surprised to see Rose upset.

"You know what I mean!" Rose scolded. "What about that letter you wrote me?"

"What about it? It was just a friendly letter."

"You helped Charles with the mules! You taught him to dance! What else did you do?" Rose glared at her.

"We were just bein' friends. There isn't much to do on the boat," said Bridget. "I thought you and I were friends, too. Why are you so huffy?"

"I am *not* huffy!" Rose put her clenched fists on her hips and stamped her foot.

"Well, you sure look huffy to me," said Bridget. "I'm goin' inside," she added as she turned and headed for the door.

Rose followed, trying to calm down. She would have to talk to Charles about that.

Uncle Dermot and Aunt Cora were saying their good-byes to Aunt Jenny and Uncle Andrew and telling them they would be back when the canal closed down for the winter.

"Get your things, Rose," boomed Uncle Dermot. "Uncle Andrew is getting the wagon and will take us down to the dock."

Rose ran upstairs, grabbed her packed carpetbag, and returned to the hall. Aunt Jenny handed her the quilt protected for the journey by a wrap of old newspapers tied with twine. Rose gave everyone another kiss, hug, and left for the wagon with the Finnegans. She looked straight ahead and made sure not to sit next to Bridget in the wagon.

When they got to the dock, Uncle Andrew helped her out of the wagon, and Uncle Dermot carried her carpetbag and quilt down to the boat. Rose lagged behind, walking along with Aunt Cora.

"What's the matter, child? You seem to be having a problem with Bridget. What did she do to you now?" Aunt Cora always seemed to know when something was wrong.

"Oh, Aunt Cora, she wrote me this letter about how she and Charles were doing all of these things together. I guess that bothered me."

Aunt Cora laughed. "Bridget and Charles. I think she exaggerated a little, maybe a lot. He did not have much to do with her the whole trip. He was doing his job and working hard."

"Really?" Rose said, her face turning red. Now she felt foolish. "But she said she taught him to dance."

"She tried to teach him to dance, he took a couple of steps, but he really wasn't interested and skedaddled."

"Oh my," said Rose. "I should have known she was exaggerating, but I reckon I sort of forgot how trying she can be." Rose felt like she had made a mountain out of a molehill.

"That she is," said Aunt Cora.

"Are you two going to get on the boat or are you going to stand there talking all day?" Uncle Dermot was anxious to get moving.

"We're coming," Aunt Cora called out.

Rose hugged her. "Thank you, Aunt Cora. I always feel better talking to you," she said.

90

"Let's get on the boat now, child. They're waiting for us," said Aunt Cora.

They picked up their long skirts and petticoats and boarded the *Flying Eagle*. Tom was on hoggee duty and got the mules going. They were on their way to Albany. It would take about four days to get there.

Rose took her carpetbag from Uncle Dermot and brought it downstairs into the cabin of the boat. She put it beside her bunk, went out of the bedchamber, and sat by the little desk in the main room. She wondered where Charles was. She did not see him when she got on the boat.

"Boo," someone yelled in her ear and hugged her. Rose nearly jumped out of her skin and when she turned to see who it was, it was him, Charles. He was standing there laughing.

"Charles, you scared the living daylights out of me," she scolded, her face turning pink.

"I'm glad you're back," he said, lowering himself into the chair next to her. "I really missed talking to you. I tried to talk to Bridget but, if truth be told, she didn't want to listen." He couldn't take his eyes off of Rose as he continued, "She just wanted to tell me what to do. She even wanted to teach me to dance." He felt like he had just escaped from jail.

Rose laughed at that. She reckoned she worried about Bridget for nothing. "I am so happy to see you," she blurted out. "I missed talking to you, too, a whole lot." Her face got a little redder, and her heartbeat quickened.

91

"The boat just wasn't the same without you." His face came alive as the words poured forth. "Well you're here now, and we have the whole trip back to talk. Don't forget you said you'd teach me how to read, and I want you to tell me all about Utica, too." He could hardly stop talking now that she was there. He wanted to tell her everything and hear all about what she had done.

"That's true," Rose beamed, "we *do* have the whole trip back to talk. And I *will* teach you how to read, and I *will* tell you all about Utica, too."

It felt so good to see Charles again and to be headed home on the *Flying Eagle*. It was going to be a delightful trip back to Albany on the Grand Canal.

1840's Sayings

all to pieces - very much, absolutely

bad egg - terrible person, good for nothing

carpetbag - a traveling bag made of leftover carpet pieces

cholera - a disease causing diarrhea and dehydration, often resulting in death within hours

cold slaw - coleslaw

conniption fit - a fit of panic

crazy as a loon - very foolish

cut shines - play tricks or jokes on someone

cyclone - something like a tornado

dashing - pleasing to the eye

do tell - tell me more

fix - trouble, problem, mess

frolic - party or celebration

hoggee - person who cares for the mules as they pull a boat down the canal, usually a boy

huffy - angry

mad as a March hare - very angry

no way, nohow - not at all

parlor - living room

pull shines - trick people

rambunctious - overexcited, troublemaking

see eye to eye - agree

shenanigans - mischief, pranks

skeer, skeered - scare someone, be frightened

smart as a steel trap - very intelligent

spirea, fraxinella - old-fashioned flowers

take a shine to - especially like someone

timid - shy, bashful

turmoil - very upset and confused

weak in the knees - feel faint

York State - New York State

Yorker - a resident of New York State

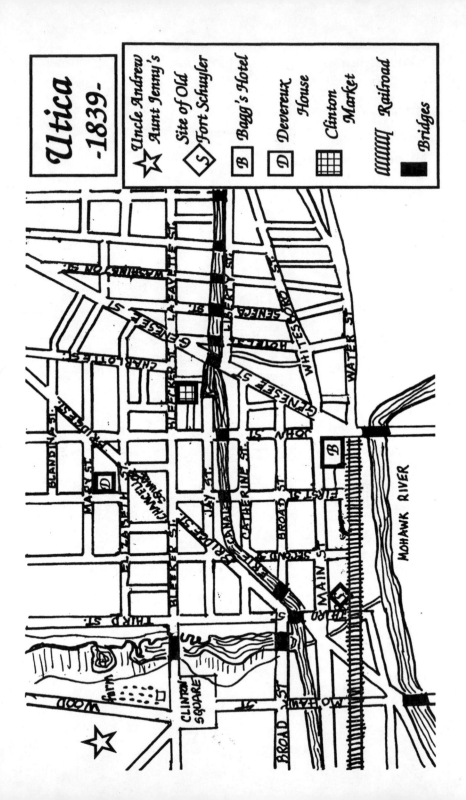

Utica -1839-

☆	Uncle Andrew Aunt Jenny's
◇ S	Site of Old Fort Schuyler
B	Bagg's Hotel
D	Devereux House
▦	Clinton Market
﹏	Railroad
■	Bridges

MOHAWK RIVER

CLINTON SQUARE

WOOD

WASHINGTON ST.
LAFAYETTE ST.
GENESEE ST.
CHARLOTTE ST.
BLEECKER ST.
SENECA ST.
HOTEL ST.
WHITESBORO ST.
WATER ST.
BLANDINA ST.
BRIDGE ST.
MARY ST.
CHANCELLOR SQUARE
ELIZABETH ST.
BLEECKER ST.
CANAL ST.
ERIE BRIDGE CANAL
JAY ST.
CATHERINE ST.
JOHN ST.
FIRST ST.
BROAD ST.
SECOND ST.
MAIN ST.
THIRD ST.
BROAD ST.
FAYETTE
FARM

Utica History and Milestones
❖ from 1758 - 1840 ❖

1758--The English build Old Fort Schuyler (presently Utica) during the French and Indian war, as one of a series of forts to protect the crossing place in the river above it. It is abandoned and left to rot, after the war.

1772--Land is sold in public auction for rent not paid by the first patent holder, William Cosby. Philip Schuyler, John Bradstreet, Rutger Bleecker, and John Scott purchase it.

1786--Three homes are located on the property. Utica gradually becomes a village consisting of two streets, Water and Main, parallel to the Mohawk River, together with a few houses on Whitestown Road.

1792--Bridge over the Mohawk River built, adding to the growth of the hamlet.

1794--Bagg's Hotel built, housing many famous guests. General Lafayette, Aaron Burr, and Washington Irving stay there.

1794, 1795, 1797--Area grows due to the road to Genesee Country

1798--April 3rd, Old Fort Schuyler is incorporated as a village in the township of Whitestown. Utica is the new name given to it.

1800--Great highway to the West is constructed which takes in Utica and bypasses Rome and Whitesboro.

1802--The Utica Aqueduct Company secures water for the village.

1805--Utica is granted its second charter.

1810-1830--Utica grows quickly, becoming the most important transportation center in the United States. Everyone thinks it will become the largest city in the country.

1817--Utica is granted a third charter and becomes a town. It is enlarged and the first directory is published. Utica Observer newspaper starts as a weekly and then in 1834 as a daily.

1819--Erie Canal between Utica and Rome opens for business.

1820--First bridges built over the Erie Canal.

1821--Saint John's Church opens on the corner of Bleecker Street and John Street.

1822--Indians migrate westward.

1825--General LaFayette visits Utica on June 10th, and has a street named after him.

1825--Entire Erie Canal from Buffalo to Albany opens for business on October 26th.

1826--Utica hosts an Erie Canal Ball in honor of the completed canal.

1827-- Slavery is abolished in New York State on July 4th.

1827--On December 28th, first street lamps, burning whale oil or kerosene, brighten Utica streets at night, lit by a lamplighter.

1832--On February 13th, Utica is incorporated as a city. The first mayor is Joseph Kirkland.

1832--In June, the Asiatic cholera epidemic enters the city of Utica with 206 ill and 65 dead. In September it is over.

1836--Chenango Canal from Utica to Binghamton opens. Railroad through Utica is completed.

1837--Massive fire destroys most of the businesses on lower Genesee Street.

1837--Business depression and financial troubles hit Utica.

1840--The legislature decides to make the Mayor's position an elected office. The first mayor elected by popular vote is John C. Devereux in 1840.

Utica in 1840

In 1840, the population of Utica was 12,782. It was known as the city of beautiful parks and was considered the crossroads of New York State. Another name for Utica was City of Trees, because of the stately elm trees lining most of the streets.

The streets themselves were neat and wide, some as much as 100 feet. Most were paved and lit, with sidewalks along them. A number of the streets were built near the Erie Canal. A majority of the buildings were brick while the others were wooden. Some of the finest houses in the New York State graced the city streets. Shops and stores lined both sides of lower Genesee Street, the business district. Many fine residential homes adorned upper Genesee Street.

Utica had 18 churches of various denominations. Some were Presbyterian, Episcopal, Dutch Reform, Baptist, Methodist, Roman Catholic, Universal, and African. Utica also boasted many charitable institutions, a County Medical Society, a Boy's Academy, a Girl's Academy, and an Exchange Building. It housed a Savings Bank, four other banks, two insurance companies and a State Lunatic Asylum.

Transportation was plentiful in the city. The Erie Canal, crossed by several stylish bridges, flowed through the center of the city. Forty-one packet boats left the city every week. The Chenango Canal built in 1836, connected Utica to Binghamton and enabled coal to be shipped from Pennsylvania to Utica. Nine stagecoach lines to all parts of the state, traveled through city. In 1836, the Utica and Schenectady Railroad opened for business.

According to the *Old Mohawk-Turnpike Book,* Utica in 1840 had: 188 retail stores, 3 lumber yards, 5 furnaces, 6 tanneries, 2 breweries, 1 flouring mill, 2 grist mills, 2 saw mills, 1 paper factory, 6 printing offices, 6 weekly newspapers, 61 brick and stone houses, 30 wooden houses, 10 academies, 36 schools, a pottery works and manufactured a lot of machinery.

Lotteries were very popular back then and served an important purpose. There were four lottery offices in Utica, the proceeds of which were used to pay for city expenses.

The mayor of Utica was John C. Devereux, the first to be elected to the office by popular vote. The common council decided that year to improve the common schools, that there should be eight of them, and put aside money for a public library as well.

Life in Utica in 1840 was typical of many cities located on the Erie Canal. The Canal brought business and prosperity to the young city. It increased the population and wealth enabling the residents to enjoy a comfortable lifestyle.

Mansion Garden Flowers

Fraxinella

Fraxinella
Perennial herb plant that gives off a flammable mist in hot weather. Usually has white flowers. Also called gas plant.

Spirea
Small to medium sized bushes that are thickly covered with small white or pink flowers falling in cascades. Member of the rose family.

Spirea

clusters

The city was considered a very refined place. There was much interest in the Arts and Cultural Events. Utica had a Museum, a Public Library, a Musical Academy, and a Mechanics Association that held lectures. The best pictures of famous American artists hung in the magnificent mansions that many very wealthy citizens built. Guests were frequently entertained in these extraordinary homes.

Farms were located on the edges of the city on Broad Street, South Street, Minden Turnpike, Columbia Street, West Street, Welch Road, Whitesboro Street, and Genesee Street above State Street. Farmers grew mostly crops of barley, rye, corn, hay, and potatoes. Apple trees, berries, a vegetable garden, and an herb garden were present on nearly all farms. Some might even have a flower garden.

Social activities included auctions, races, frolics, all kinds of "bees", state and county fairs, and air balloon rides. In the winter, sleigh riding, parties, potluck suppers, and ice-skating on the canal, provided more outings for Utica citizens.

Sources

Bagg, Dr. Moses M. **Memorial History of Utica: From Its Settlement to the Present Time.** Syracuse, NY: D. Mason and Company, 1892

Bagg, Dr. Moses M. **Pioneers of Utica.** Utica, NY: Curtis and Childs, 1877

Clarke, T. Wood M.D. **Utica for a Century and a Half.** Utica, NY: The Widtman Press, 1952

Ellis, David M. **The Upper Mohawk Country: An Illustrated History of Greater Utica.** Windsor, CA: Windsor Publications, 1982

Greene, Nelson. **Old Mohawk Turnpike Book.** Fort Plain, NY: Journal and Courier Press, 1924

Hendricks, Ulysses Prentice. **A History of Agriculture in New York State.** New York: Hill and Yang, 1933

McCutcheon, Marc. **Everyday Life in the 1800s.** Cincinnati, OH: Writer's Digest Books, 1993

Miller, Blandina Dudley. **A Sketch of Old Utica.** Utica, NY: Fierstine Printing House, 1896

New Century Club of Utica. **Outline History of the City of Utica.** Utica, NY: L. C. Childs and Son, 1900